SPONGEBOB SQUAREPANTS

SPONGEBOB TEES OFF

by Ilanit Oliver
illustrated by Stephen Reed

Simon Spotlight/Nickelodeon
New York London Toronto Sydney New Delhi

Stephen Hillenburg (signature)

Based on the TV series *SpongeBob SquarePants*™ created by Stephen Hillenburg as seen on Nickelodeon™

SIMON SPOTLIGHT/NICKELODEON

An imprint of Simon & Schuster Children's Publishing Division

1230 Avenue of the Americas, New York, New York 10020

© 2012 Viacom International Inc. All rights reserved. NICKELODEON, *SpongeBob SquarePants*,

and all related titles, logos, and characters are trademarks of Viacom International Inc. Created by Stephen Hillenburg.

All rights reserved, including the right of reproduction in whole or in part in any form.

SIMON SPOTLIGHT and colophon are registered trademarks of Simon & Schuster, Inc.

For information about special discounts for bulk purchases, please contact Simon & Schuster Special Sales at 1-866-506-1949 or business@simonandschuster.com.

Manufactured in the United States of America 1211 LAK

First Edition 10 9 8 7 6 5 4 3 2 1

ISBN 978-1-4424-3617-6

"Hey, Squidward, watch this!" SpongeBob called from inside the Krusty Krab kitchen. "I'm going to make this patty bounce off the refrigerator, fly through that hoop, and land right on the grill!"

"I don't care," Squidward croaked.

"Woo-hoo!" SpongeBob called. "I got a hole in one!"

The patty had bounced, flown, and landed smack dab in the middle of the grill. *FSSS!*

"SpongeBob, I'm trying to watch TV," Squidward whined.

Just then Squidward's program was interrupted by the famous news anchor Perch Perkins. "The mayor has announced that the town will host its first-ever charity golf tournament, the Bikini Bottom Classic, with the world-famous golfer Annika Swordfish.

"This Saturday, one lucky citizen will get to play against her in a friendly game! All proceeds go toward fixing up Bikini Bottom's public library. Enter for your chance to play at the Krusty Krab this Thursday night!"

"Ahh! Annika Swordfish is coming here!" SpongeBob shrieked. "I have to win that contest and show her what I can do!"

On Thursday night all of Bikini Bottom was at the Krusty Krab.

"This place is just burstin' with people ready to hand over their money!" Mr. Krabs cried out. "This tournament is the best thing that ever happened to me restaurant!"

The mayor stepped up to the giant glass bowl full of names and pulled one out. "And the winner is . . . SpongeBob SquarePants!"

SpongeBob was so happy, he jumped and accidentally flung his spatula. The patty he'd been flipping sailed across the room, right into the bowl of leftover names.

"Now that's the kind of arm you'll need to have on Saturday!" Patrick called out.

"Uh, Patrick," SpongeBob said, "you've got the wrong sport. I won't be *throwing* the ball. I'll be swinging my club at it."

"Which, of course, you'll need your arms for," Patrick noted.

The day before the tournament SpongeBob went to practice. He wanted to make sure his hips were squared off and his grip was perfect.

"Come on, SpongeBob! Knock the ball out of the park!" Patrick cheered.

"Uh, Patrick, I think the goal is to keep the ball on the green," SpongeBob told him.

"Whatever helps you focus, buddy. Think you can do it?"

"I don't *think*, Patrick. I *know*!"

"Good for you," Patrick replied. "I don't think either!"

18

SpongeBob swung his club, and the ball went rolling across the bridge, over the fence, and straight into the eighteenth hole.

"You're going to sweep Annika away tomorrow!" Patrick said.

SpongeBob shrugged. "I just want to raise enough money to repair the library. And if big golf is anything like miniature golf, I won't miss a hole!"

On Saturday morning SpongeBob woke up early, got dressed in his best golf outfit, and rushed over to Patrick's rock.

Patrick was all ready. "SpongeBob," he said, "as your caddy, I must insist that I carry your club this instant!"

"What's a caddy?" SpongeBob asked.

"I just told you," Patrick insisted. "It's the person who carries your club."

So Patrick grabbed SpongeBob's lone club and off they went.

At the Bikini Bottom Shell Club the grounds of the golf course were newly groomed and excitement was in the air. Townspeople, fans, TV crews, and photographers had gathered to see Annika Swordfish. Everyone wanted to get a picture or, better yet, an interview! There were even some stars, like Grubby Grouper, Jessica Albacore, and Justin Beardfish, who had come to watch the tournament.

"Thank you all for coming to our first-ever Bikini Bottom Classic," the mayor said. "And thank you, Annika Swordfish, for joining us. All the proceeds from today's event will go to our library, so please buy lots of stuff! Now let the game begin!"

SpongeBob and Annika shook hands and then walked off together toward the tee box.

"I'm a big fan, Ms. Swordfish," SpongeBob said.

Annika smiled. "Thank you, SpongeBob, but please, call me Annika. I'm looking forward to playing with you!"

Soak Up the Win, SpongeBob!

Annika Will Fillet the Course!

Annika Rules the Green!

Today Green YELLOW

Annika

Annika

NGEBOB

ONGEBOB

As they walked, SpongeBob realized he couldn't see an obstacle for what seemed like miles!

"Hey, Patrick," he whispered. "Where are all the windmills and castles?"

"Oh, big golf doesn't have any of those," Patrick replied.

"*No obstacles!*" SpongeBob shouted so loud that everyone looked at him. He quickly covered up, "Heh-heh, I mean, no obstacle will hold me back from playing my best!"

SpongeBob also noticed that Annika's caddy was carrying a lot of different clubs. "Why does Annika have so many clubs?" SpongeBob asked Patrick.

"Unlike miniature golf, big golf requires a few clubs," Patrick explained. "There are woods, wedges, irons, and putters. Woods include the driver and fairway woods—"

"Uh-huh . . . ," SpongeBob said, "but where are all the holes? They must be miles apart!"

"Right again!" Patrick replied. "Everything in big golf is bigger than it is in miniature golf: the grounds, the fairway, and even the swings!"

Finally it was time to tee off. Annika went first. She asked her caddy for a driver and then took her swing. Her ball went flying at least two hundred yards across the fairway. SpongeBob was so shocked, his jaw dropped to the ground and his eyes nearly popped out of his head.

Then it was SpongeBob's turn. He lifted his club and swung. The ball rolled gently and stopped a few feet away from the tee. The crowd gasped.

"Swing bigger!" Patrick whispered.

"But what if my ball rolls into one of those sandy spaces? Or worse, it lands in the water?" SpongeBob asked nervously. "How will I keep my score low?"

"Don't worry," Patrick replied. "Even the scores are bigger in big golf! The more swings you take, the higher your score!"

Overjoyed, SpongeBob let his swing go wild, and by the ninth hole, his score was already 72! Annika's score was only 30.

"SpongeBob, you're getting incredible distance out of that putter!" Annika remarked, watching his ball roll past the thirteenth hole and land in the sand bunker.

"Really?" SpongeBob said, excited. "Thanks! Your swings are unbeatable! But based on my score, I'd say my club and I are doing all right. Wouldn't you?" he added with a wink.

Then he hunkered down to hit his ball out of the sand.

On the sidelines the crowd had almost tripled in size.

"Whoa, the crowd has gotten huge!" SpongeBob said on their walk to the sixteenth hole.

"Well, this is quite an event," Annika answered.

"It sure is! You're the best player in the world!" SpongeBob said. Then he nudged Patrick. "But I'm giving her a good fight, huh, Pat?"

"You sure are, buddy! I've never seen a score as high as yours."

BIKINI BOTTOM
C·L·A·S·S·I·C

| A. SWORDFISH | 59 |
| S. SQUAREPANTS | 133 |

On the eighteenth hole, SpongeBob dented his putter trying to hit his ball out of the rough—*again*. A wave of whispers fluttered through the crowd of onlookers. What was SpongeBob going to do?

"Here," Annika said, handing him a seven iron. "Try this one."

SpongeBob took the club back to his ball in the rough. He hit the ball, and it went flying across the fairway and straight onto the green, landing only a few inches away from the hole!

"Great shot, SpongeBob!" Annika cheered. "When you use the right club you actually have a nice swing."

"You really think so?" SpongeBob asked.

Annika nodded. "And if you putt well, you could finish this hole with one more shot."

"But finishing in one shot would mean a lower score," SpongeBob said. "And I need a really big score so lots of money will be donated to the library."

"I'm sorry, SpongeBob, but in golf, the *lowest* score wins the game," Annika explained.

SpongeBob couldn't believe his ears. The scoring was one thing that was the same in big golf *and* miniature golf—and he blew it! "Are you saying that my score of 156 is the biggest *losing* score of all time?"

"I'm afraid so," Annika confirmed.

SpongeBob sank the ball smoothly in one shot, but it didn't matter. With a score of 67, Annika won the Bikini Bottom Classic by a landslide. The crowd cheered excitedly for the famous golfer.

Poor SpongeBob was miserable. "I'm sorry I let Bikini Bottom down," he told the mayor. "I know my score didn't raise enough money for the library."

Bikini Bottom
Public Library   Saturday

$8,000,000,000,000

Eight Trillion Dollars and $\frac{00}{100}$

memo: Golf Tournament   Mr. Mayor

"SpongeBob, what are you talking about?" the mayor said. "The town loves you! This has been the most entertaining game of golf they've ever seen. Because of that, the library has received more than enough donations to be completely rebuilt. So . . . thank *you!*"

"See, SpongeBob," Patrick said, throwing his arm around his best friend. "I told you that you'd hit the ball out of the park!"

"I hit it out of the park all right," SpongeBob agreed, "and out of the sand and out of the water!"

And with that the two friends laughed the whole way home.